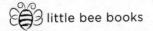 little bee books

An imprint of Bonnier Publishing USA
251 Park Avenue South, New York, NY 10010
Copyright © 2019 by Bonnier Publishing USA
All rights reserved, including the right of reproduction in whole or in part in any form. Little Bee Books is a trademark of Bonnier Publishing USA, and associated colophon is a trademark of Bonnier Publishing USA.

Library of Congress Cataloging-in-Publication Data is available upon request.

Manufactured in China   TPL 1118
ISBN 978-1-4998-0834-6 (PBK)
First Edition 10 9 8 7 6 5 4 3 2 1
ISBN 978-1-4998-0835-3 (HC)
First Edition 10 9 8 7 6 5 4 3 2 1
littlebeebooks.com
bonnierpublishingusa.com

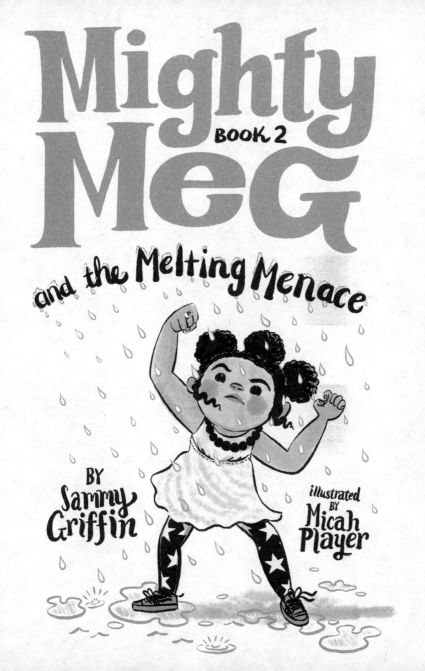

Mighty Meg

BOOK 2

Meg

and the Melting Menace

BY
Sammy Griffin

illustrated BY
Micah Player

Contents

Chapter One: In the Hot Seat at Dinner.......1

Chapter Two: Hiding from Mom............ 13

Chapter Three: A Field of Icicles........... 21

Chapter Four: Melting Danger 29

Chapter Five: Super Secrets 35

Chapter Six: Hiding out in the Library 43

Chapter Seven: Questions in 53
   Science Class

Chapter Eight: Hall Pass 63

Chapter Nine: Super Sneaky...............73

Chapter Ten: Caught Speeding Home 81

Chapter One:
In the Hot Seat at Dinner

Meg snuck in through the side door of her house. She hung her jacket on a hook and kicked her shoes off in the mudroom.

"Meg?" Mom called from the kitchen.

She had hoped to make it to her room before anyone realized she was home. "Hi, Mom!" Meg walked over to where her mom stood by the stove, flipping grilled cheeses.

"How was school today, honey?" Mom looked tired. Her feet were bare, but she still wore her grey business jacket and skirt.

Meg leaned in for a half hug as Mom used the spatula in her free hand to flip grilled cheese sandwiches. "Good."

"What have you and the girls been up to?" Mom asked. "You haven't said much about Ruby and Tara lately."

The past week, Meg had been testing her new superpowers after school. She practiced in the open field by her house, using her super-speed to run around the field, her super-strength to lift heavy rocks, and her heightened senses to see and hear faraway animals. She was even working on controlling her invisibility, so she would stop turning invisible whenever she was scared. Meg hadn't been to either of her friends' houses to do homework with them like usual, but Mom didn't know that.

Meg shrugged. "Um . . . not much."

"Why don't you and Curtis set the table, and we'll talk more about your day over dinner."

Meg groaned to herself. She would have to figure out a way to get her brother to do all the talking. *Dinosaurs!* She smiled. If she asked Curtis about *Velociraptors*, he would talk all night.

"Curtis!" Meg called her brother away from the TV in the living room. He reluctantly stood and came into the kitchen to help, the sound from his nature program still blaring in the background.

DAWN OF THE CHICKEN O SAURUS?

As Meg handed him the plates, he asked, "Did you know some scientists want to create a *Chickenosaurus*?" Curtis spent the next ten minutes talking about how cool a chicken-dinosaur would be. By the time he had turned off the television and sat down to eat, he was dinosaured out.

Mom ladled soup into their bowls and passed around the plate of grilled cheese sandwiches. Before anyone had even taken a bite, Curtis turned all the attention back to Meg as he said, "On my way to Homework Club today, I saw Tara and Ruby leave school without Meg." He slurped up a spoonful of soup, leaving a thick red mustache on his lip.

"Manners." Mom pushed Curtis's napkin toward him before turning to Meg. "Where were you, sweetie?"

Meg's cheeks flushed as she thought back to an afternoon spent jumping up into the tallest branches of the oak tree in the field by their house. It may sound like an easy feat for someone with superpowers, but apparently her super-jumping abilities did not come with super-coordination.

Meg had been practicing jumping all week, but it still took her quite a few tries to stick the landings.

"Looking for a book at the library," Meg lied, staring at her soup as if it was the most interesting thing she'd ever seen.

"Oh, really?" Mom swallowed a spoonful of soup before asking, "What book?"

"I didn't actually find it." Meg pulled at the crust on her sandwich. "It's a new book in a series, and the school doesn't have it yet."

"Ah, that's too bad," Mom said, and then she asked Curtis what he was reading in school these days.

Meg relaxed back into her seat, happy to have all the attention diverted away from her. But then she realized how easily Mom had believed her lie, and she felt even worse.

Chapter Two:
Hiding from Mom

After they cleaned up dinner and Mom signed her homework folder, Meg got ready for bed. She was in the bathroom brushing her teeth when Mom passed by on her way to Curtis's room. "I can't wait to hear about this new book when I tuck you into bed!"

Meg stood with her foamy mouth hanging open, toothbrush still in hand. What was she going to talk about? She glanced at her magical ring before she spat and rinsed, and then stared at her reflection again. If Mom found out about the ring and her superpowers, she would take it all away. Even if Meg wanted to use them to help people in trouble, Mom would still think it was too dangerous.

She could hear Mom's muffled voice down the hall reading a bedtime story to Curtis. Meg tiptoed out of the bathroom and into her own room. The bright yellow paint and ruffly bedspread always relaxed her. This was Meg's safe and happy place, no matter what happened outside her bedroom door. She lay down on her bed and stretched out, tracing the plastic stars on the ceiling with her eyes.

"Good night, C." Meg heard Mom begin her nightly tucking-in ritual with Curtis. She imagined her turning on his night-light and blowing him a kiss before heading down the hall to Meg's room. Mom would bombard her with questions that Meg could only answer with lies.

The knot in her stomach returned and Meg looked down to find she had completely vanished! She still couldn't choose when she turned invisible. In fact, she had almost no control over when it happened at all! Mom walked through the doorway, and Meg watched her step into her room and check all the corners for her.

"Meg?" Mom put her hands on her hips and cocked her head to the side, her eyebrows bunched together in confusion. "Where did you get to now?"

Mom swept about the room, her robe catching air and looking like a cape blowing out from behind her. "Meg? Where are you, sweetie?" Mom's footsteps padded through the house and Meg climbed under her covers and concentrated on becoming visible again.

During her superpower practices earlier that week, she had discovered that when she turned invisible, if she imagined being visible in her mind, it made it easier for her to become visible in real life. Her fingers wiggled before her eyes, and Meg released a long sigh.

"Meghan Asha Hughes!" Mom sounded frustrated now. "Where are you?!"

Meg turned toward the wall and closed her eyes. She could avoid all Mom's questions if she pretended to be asleep when she was found in her bed.

Meg could hear Mom's footsteps as she walked down the hall and entered her room.

Mom whispered, "Well, I'll be darned."
She silently moved through her tucking-in
ritual with Meg, bringing the covers up over
her shoulders and kissing her on the cheek
before whispering, "Sleep tight, my strong
and wise warrior."

Meg couldn't help but smile as Mom
walked out of her room. It was as if Mom's
nighttime blessing had come true.

Chapter Three:
A Field of Icicles

Curtis was antsy that morning, bouncing in his seat as he shoveled cereal into his mouth.

"Slow down, C." Mom watched him from the kitchen as she stood by the toaster, waiting for her bread to pop.

Meg pulled the crust from her honey toast and crumbled it over her scrambled eggs while Curtis scrunched his face at her plate. "That's gross," he said, his mouth full of mushy Sweet Flakes.

"*That* is disgusting," Meg responded, rolling her eyes and pointing at his bad table manners. Maybe he would be more respectable when he turned eight.

"I want to get to school early today," Curtis said. "There's a tetherball championship, and I'm going to win it."

"Oh, are you now?" Mom sat at the table with her coffee and toast. "Then you two better hustle!"

Curtis dashed from the dining room, and Meg knew that was her cue to hurry up and finish breakfast. She didn't want her brother nagging her to leave.

By the time Mom had cleaned up Curtis's breakfast, they were all ready to walk out the door. Curtis rushed ahead. Meg grabbed her sack lunch and her backpack as she ran to catch up, careful not to use her super-speed where someone could see her. They both blew Mom kisses as they passed the driveway and jogged down the sidewalk.

Once they were out of sight, Meg used her super-speed to catch up with her brother. In a flash, she was right behind him. He never even saw her coming.

"Whoa, when did you catch up?" he asked.

Before she could answer, Curtis stopped. They had reached the spot where Meg had been hiding out after school that week, practicing her superpowers. But instead of an open field, the tall grass was covered in icy spikes! They looked like stalagmites, those rock formations that rose from the bottom of caves like spears. These jagged pieces of ice were nearly as tall as Curtis.

"What are those?" Curtis asked.

"I don't know." Meg thought back to the geyser that had flooded the stream, and the glowing moths she'd seen last week. "This makes no sense. It's too warm for ice."

Small puddles were already forming around the snowy cones as they melted in the new-day sunlight. Meg guessed that they would be gone by lunchtime.

"Hey! You're going to miss the tournament."
She nudged Curtis, who blinked hard before
snapping out of his trance.

"That's right!" Curtis squared his backpack
and took off running for school.

With her super-speed, it didn't take much
for her to keep up with him, and as she ran,
Meg's concern about the strangle icicles
continued to needle at the back of her mind.

Chapter Four:
Melting Danger

Meg and Curtis traveled down the shortcut that led to the playground behind their school. It was a narrow dirt path lined with trees. Normally, the sun shone through the leaves and it was a pretty walk. But today the path was really foggy. Curtis had to look down at his feet to make sure he didn't trip. He could barely see in front of his face.

As they passed through an opening in the fence, the fog lifted and Curtis saw a crowd gathered around the tetherball courts. He took off running. Meg watched him go, standing on the spot where the dirt path turned to pavement.

Something about the fog just wasn't right. Meg used her super-sight to peer through it. Usually the barrier next to the path was steep and layered with stones, but with her powers, Meg could see that the stones were being held up by a thick ice shelf! It was as if a troll or goblin had created the perfect booby trap, stacking the stones behind a melting wall. And just like the field of snowy spikes, the ice was slowly thawing. A trickle of water was already flowing onto the path in front of her.

Meg studied the ice shelf, just as puzzled by it as she had been by the icy stalagmites earlier. Why would there be strange ice formations in two different places this close to spring? Regardless of what had caused the ice to appear, once the ice melted, the stones would topple onto the path. Anyone traveling on the shortcut to or from school could get hurt!

No one would even be able to see the danger through the fog. Meg thought about telling a teacher, so they could just shut down the path. But how could she explain that she could see the ice shelf without revealing that she had super-sight? If only she could break the ice, causing the rocks to fall harmlessly while no one was around. Meg bent her legs, ready to leap into action, but kids began walking down the path. The shortcut would be crowded with students until school started.

She would have to solve this problem another time.

Chapter Five: Super Secrets

Meg waited on a bench outside the front of the school until Tara's dad pulled into the drop-off lane and let her friends out. For as long as Meg could remember, she and Ruby had been like sisters separated by three blocks. And when Tara moved onto Ruby's street in the second grade, they all began hanging out together and had been best friends ever since.

Sometimes Tara's and Ruby's parents drove them to school while Meg walked with Curtis. After waving goodbye to Tara's dad, Tara and Ruby skipped down the walkway with their arms locked together. Meg felt jealous, knowing they'd been spending time without her after school all week. Even though she knew it was her choice and not theirs, she still felt sad.

"Meg!" The girls called out to her and ran to the bench.

Meg forced a smile and gave them both a big hug.

"We've missed you." Ruby looped her arm through Meg's so she could join their chain.

"Yeah!" Tara agreed. "We were starting to worry that turning eight had made you too cool for us."

"I've just been busy after school lately,"
Meg said. "That's all."

"We're just kidding, Meg." Ruby bumped
shoulders with her so she'd know they were
playing. "But we're dying to know what you've
been up to!"

"Definitely!" Tara leaned over to meet Meg's eyes. "It has to be more exciting than homework and no-bake cookies." Being reminded of their after-school routine made Meg feel a little homesick, even though she hadn't really gone anywhere.

"Not really," Meg said, even though what she had been doing instead of hanging out with her friends had been pretty exciting. Keeping this super secret from her friends made her feel even worse, and Meg started looking forward to the first bell.

The girls walked into the school together, their footsteps echoing in the foyer.

"You can tell us all about it at lunch," Ruby said.

Tara nearly cut Ruby off when she added, "We're going to blast you with questions so we don't miss anything!" Both her fists splayed when she said blast, like she was making explosions with her hands.

Meg laughed nervously as they turned down the third-grade hallway. All of these questions were making her anxious. First her mom, now her friends—it was hard keeping secrets. Concentrating on being visible, Meg wondered how she could avoid answering their questions while still working on a solution for the melting ice. Spending lunch in the library might help solve both problems.

Chapter Six:
Hiding out in the Library

If she stood on her tiptoes and looked out the back window of the library, with her super-sight, Meg could just barely see the ice shelf. It had already melted halfway, and a few stones had fallen onto the path. At this rate, the ice would break away just as kids were walking home!

"Meg, sweetie," Mrs. Johansen called to her from the checkout desk. The library was empty, and they were the only two people in the room. "You don't want to eat lunch with your class?"

Kids could eat lunch in the library if Mrs. Johansen was there. The librarian was one of the nicest people Meg knew, and she had bright blue eyes and long white hair. She sometimes wore her glasses like a necklace, attached to a string of colorful beads.

It was Mrs. Johansen's idea to open the library during lunch, so all kids felt like they had a quiet and safe place to eat and spend recess if they wanted. Meg nodded in response to Mrs. Johansen's question and held up her lunch bag as if it were proof.

Meg sat down and pulled her peanut butter and honey sandwich from the bag. She needed to figure out how to destroy the ice shelf and the threat of a stone avalanche before lunch was over.

Meg scribbled down ideas as she ate, crowding a small slip of paper with mostly silly solutions. Her plan had to be perfect: She needed to get onto the playground, fix the ice shelf while no one was on the path, and then come back, all unnoticed. She tapped the pencil to her temple as she thought.

48

"Got it!" she whispered. She jumped up and went to the nonfiction section of the library, searching for just the right book. When she found the one she wanted, she took it over to the checkout desk.

"A book on ice? In the springtime? That's an interesting choice," Mrs. Johansen said, stamping the inside before handing the book back to Meg.

The first bell rang as Meg returned to her table in the back. She threw away her trash before quietly opening the back window and leaving her library book on the window ledge. Meg took a deep breath. *This had better work*, she thought.

Chapter Seven:
Questions in Science Class

Meg nearly collided with Tara and Ruby as she darted from the library into the science classroom after lunch.

"Hey, where were you?" Ruby asked, her mouth pouty.

"Yeah." Tara looked annoyed. Of the three girls, she had the shortest fuse, although she was also the quickest to stand up for her friends. "We looked all over for you."

"Sorry," Meg said, and she meant it. She didn't want to upset Tara and Ruby. "I had to do some research at the library."

Luckily, there wasn't much time to talk before the bell rang and science class started. Tara and Ruby both turned away from Meg to face the front of the class, but their frustration hung in the air like an invisible cloud.

Mr. Fester paced the front of the classroom as he continued their discussion from yesterday about strange natural phenomena, like fire tornadoes, underwater crop circles, and sailing desert stones that left long trails behind them in the sand. Of all the science teachers Meg had ever known, Mr. Fester looked the most like a science teacher from a TV show: He wore glasses with thick, dark frames, had curly red hair, and wore collared shirts with pockets full of writing utensils.

This couldn't be more perfect, Meg thought. Her hand shot up into the air.

"Meg?"

"What about a field of icicles. Could that be a thing?"

Meg could hear a handful of students behind her snickering at her question.

"Actually." Mr. Fester stopped and nodded his head thoughtfully. "It *is* a thing. Only they're not called icicles, but *penitentes*."

"Penny-what?" someone called from the back of the room.

"Pen-i-ten-teys." Mr. Fester sounded the word out slowly. "*Penitente* is the Spanish word for penitent, which means someone who is sorry for something. People thought these icy formations looked like a group of people praying for forgiveness."

He rushed to the tablet on his desk, which was connected to the whiteboard, and searched for pictures. He showed images of the same thing Meg and Curtis had seen that morning: fields of jagged ice cones pointed at the sun.

"They occur in high altitudes when dew forms, but temperatures are below freezing." Mr. Fester had stopped on one picture where the white *penitente* stood out against a bright blue sky. He gestured at the picture enthusiastically. "The sun turns sections of the snow into vapor without melting, leaving behind the formations you see. Some of these snow spikes can be as tall as thirteen feet."

The ones Meg and Curtis saw had not even been half that tall, although they may have started out taller and melted down. Also, Plainview was in a valley, not a high altitude place at all. Not to mention, it was not very cold. It was nearly spring! *Penitentes* in Plainview sounded practically impossible.

Jackson, seated behind Meg, groaned as Mr. Fester went on. "*Penitentes* are found mostly in South America—this is a picture from the Andes Mountains. Can you see how they look a bit like people praying?"

"Brainiac." Jackson leaned forward to whisper into Meg's ear. "You better *pray* he's almost done answering your boring question."

Meg sank into her seat as Mr. Fester droned on.

Chapter Eight:
Hall Pass

After showing a video on the northern lights, Mr. Fester assigned a short worksheet for students to complete by the end of class. Meg knew this was her best chance to sneak out to stop the ice shelf from causing an avalanche!

She asked Mr. Fester if she could go to the bathroom, and he gave her a hall pass. Meg snuck back into the library where Mrs. Johansen stood at her desk giving the second graders a lesson on genres, the different types of stories you could read.

The librarian was so fascinated with her topic that Meg was able to slip into the back of the group and blend in with the class. When Mrs. Johansen turned her back to grab sample books to show the students, Meg tiptoed backward until she could duck between a row of books and eventually crawl to the window she'd left open during lunch.

Waiting until just the right moment, when Mrs. Johansen and the second  graders were completely distracted, Meg climbed onto the windowsill and popped the screen out from the  window. Placing her legs through first, Meg sat on the ledge. With a little grace, she dropped from the second-floor opening and landed on her feet with a thud. She didn't have much time to lose.

Meg sprinted toward the ice shelf. It had nearly dripped away to release the stones, which now tottered on a thin sheet of ice. With her super-sight, she could see a man through the fog. He was speed-walking at the far end of the path. Meg had to act fast. She had already been gone from class for too long. How was she going to clear the path?

On the other side of the rocks, away from the path, she spotted a canal. If she could make the rocks fall that way, the danger would be gone. Searching for something to help her, she found a wooden post lining the shortcut.

Like a professional weight lifter, Meg pulled the wooden post from the earth and hoisted it above her head. Holding it high, and ignoring the worms and bugs that dropped down from it, she jumped over the stones to the top of the ice shelf. She nearly lost her balance on its slippery surface.

Meg found herself wishing again that super-coordination was a part of her superhero package.

Carefully, she turned around and faced the stones being held back by the ice. Using the post like a plow, Meg bulldozed the stones down off the shelf and into the canal on the other side. When she turned back around to admire her work, she saw that only a few small rocks were now dotting the path. The shortcut was safe again!

The man coming down the path would be able to see her soon. Luckily, he was concentrating on the ground as he drew closer. Before he looked up, Meg sped away.

Meg darted back through the playground at super-speed, right up to the library window she had slipped through minutes earlier.

Chapter Nine:
Super Sneaky

Meg climbed up the wall so she could peek into the library through the open window. Mrs. Johansen stood at the desk, checking out the second graders' books.

While Mrs. Johansen was busy, Meg shimmied through the window.

After she snuck inside, Meg put the window screen back on, pulled the hall pass from her back pocket, grabbed the library book from the ledge, and walked toward the library doors.

As she passed the front desk, Mrs. Johansen's head snapped her way and the librarian called out, "Meg? When did you come in here?"

This had all been part of Meg's plan. In response to Mrs. Johansen, Meg held her hall pass up in one hand and the library book in the other. "I forgot my book," she said.

The librarian nodded and called after Meg on her way out the door, "See you later!"

As Meg turned the corner heading back to science class, she practically collided with Mr. Fester. He let out a whoop of surprise before he said, "I was just coming to find you. You've been gone for a while, Meg. Are you feeling okay?"

"Yep." She smiled, and then showed him the library book, called *Strange Frozen Phenomena*. "Sorry. I was really curious about the ice formations we talked about in class." And for once, she wasn't lying! Meg still wanted to know how ice had formed in Plainview at the start of spring.

"I'll let it go this time," Mr. Fester said with a relaxed sigh. Meg could tell he was pleased at her interest in his lecture that afternoon. "But next time, you need permission to go to the library."

"Thank you, Mr. Fester," she said, and led the way back to class.

Meg was relieved that she had solved the melting ice problem, but she still had one more super task she had to complete by the end of the day.

HONESTY IS THE BEST POLICY

Chapter Ten:
Caught Speeding Home

When the final bell rang after her last class, Meg rushed to her cubby in the hallway. Lately, she had been grabbing her backpack and speeding away from the school before her friends had a chance to see her leave. But today was different. Instead of running away from Tara and Ruby, she was trying to find them.

She waited by Ruby's cubby outside Mr. Fester's class, where the girls used to meet before Meg had gotten her superpowers. Ruby's name sparkled above her cubby, cut out from purple construction paper and dusted with gold glitter.

Soon, Tara and Ruby walked from their classroom into the hallway, laughing with their heads ducked together. Meg felt worried as she watched them, but then she reminded herself that *she* had left her friends; they hadn't left her.

When the girls saw Meg, they both stopped and stared.

Tara folded her arms across her chest, still looking annoyed that Meg had avoided them at lunch. "Oh, you're here. What's wrong?" she asked.

"Nothing," Meg said, picking at the strap on her backpack before looking at her friends. "I was just hoping I could hang out with you guys after school today."

Tara relaxed, and her arms dropped down to her sides. Ruby squealed and pulled Meg into a crushing hug. "Of course you can! It hasn't been the same without you!"

Tara joined in, and the three friends jumped up and down in their little huddle.

After the girls spent the afternoon making no-bake cookies and working on their homework at Tara's house, Meg started her four-block walk home. The big smile that had been on her face since school let out made her cheeks ache.

Meg tightened the straps on her backpack and looked around to see if anyone was watching. The sun had dipped below the tree line, and the cool air bit at her fingers and nose. She zipped her jacket up all the way and waited for a car to pass before she took off down the road, running so fast, the air whizzed in her ears.

Mom and Curtis pulled into the driveway just as Meg was jogging up the steps to the house. She stopped and waited for them to catch up.

As Mom stepped closer, Meg noticed that Mom looked at her differently, almost like Meg was an exhibit at the zoo. "Since when did you become an Olympic runner?" she asked suspiciously.

Meg looked down at her orange sneakers and her cheeks prickled with heat. "I've always liked to run." While that was true, Meg couldn't help but wonder how much her mother had seen.

"I stopped by Tara's house to pick you up a few minutes ago, but she said you'd left." Mom unlocked the door and waved Meg and Curtis inside ahead of her. "They were surprised you weren't still on their block since you'd just barely started walking home."

Meg shrugged and kept walking past Mom. "I'm going to put my backpack away," she said, turning to look at Mom before heading up to her room. The suspicious look from before had been replaced with a smile.

"Hurry back for dinner," Mom said as Meg skipped off with her backpack.

After she ducked into the safety of her bedroom, she dropped her backpack on the floor. Meg would have to be much more careful from now on.

She admired the scarlet ring on her finger and smiled to herself. She had saved people from getting hurt on the shortcut today, and that left a happy, warm feeling in her chest. Meg spun in a circle before collapsing onto her bed.

Maybe she could handle this superhero thing after all.

STRANGE
FROZEN
PHENOMENA

Mighty Meg
BOOK 3

and the Accidental Nemesis

BY
Sammy
Griffin

illustrated
BY
Micah
Player

Chapter One:
Early-Morning Fright-ball

Meg and Curtis stood at the back edge of their school's fence, studying the playground with their feet planted and arms across their chests. The sun was rising in the sky, but the air was still cool enough to bite at their bare skin. The bell would ring soon, but there was still time before school started, and they each needed to decide where they would play.

Curtis eyed the three four-square courts busy with games and a short line where kids waited their turns. In the middle of the field, third and fourth graders played touch football, while a small crowd scampered over the playground in a race that seemed to end by touching the top of the climbing wall.

"I'm going over there." Curtis pointed at

the football kids running toward the bench they were using as one of their goalposts.

"No way." Meg swung her arm out to hold him back. "Those are big kids playing football, and you're just going to get hurt."

"I'm a big kid!" Curtis said, but hung back anyway. "And you're not the boss of me."

"You're six." Meg walked toward the playground, making sure her little brother kept pace with her. "And I am the boss of you when we're at school. Mom said so."

Curtis grumbled as they marched around the huddle at the edge of the field. Jackson stood in the middle, giving his teammates instructions. "We're gonna cream 'em!" he yelled, and the small group of kids around him cheered. They ran back toward the other team, lining up in the middle of the field.

Curtis took off toward the slide, and Meg

went to the front of the obstacle course, hoping to join the next race. As she waited, Meg played with the magical ring sitting on her finger and wondered if she could win the race without using her super-speed. She watched as the touch football game started again. Jackson took the snap. He ignored his teammates who were waving their arms for him to pass it. Instead, he took the ball and ran it down the field. He dodged through the other team, most of them looking confused, like they weren't really sure how to play football after all.

As he neared the bench goalpost, Tommy Hedrich from Meg's reading class stepped into Jackson's path, both arms raised to try and tag him. But instead of slowing down, Jackson sped up, like Tommy was the finish line tape he had to bust through. Even though they were far away, Meg could tell that if neither boy backed down, someone was going to get hurt.

Meg ran from the playland, kicking up dirt as she zipped to the field using enough of her super-speed to get there quickly, but not enough to draw extra attention to herself. The other players slowed her down as she wove around them to stop any collision. Meg got there just in time to see Jackson ram Tommy with his shoulder.

The smaller boy crumpled to the ground in a heap, Jackson landing heavily on top of him. Tommy yelled out in pain, and the teacher on duty blew her whistle and ran over to check on him.

It took a few minutes, but Meg and the teacher finally helped Tommy up. As soon as he stepped onto his right leg, he cried out in pain. Two of Tommy's friends slung his arms over their shoulders and walked him to the nurse's office while Jackson kicked at the grass, moving the football from one hand to the other.

"Jackson," the teacher snapped. "You know we only play touch football. What you did was very dangerous. Come with me to the principal's office."

Sammy Griffin is a children's book author and super-geek who fangirls over superheroes and comic books in real life. She lives in Idaho Falls, Idaho, with her super-geek family.

Micah Player was born in Alaska and now lives in the mountains of Utah with a schoolteacher named Stephanie. They are the parents of two rad kids, one brash Yorkshire terrier, and several Casio keyboards.

micahplayer.com

Journey to some magical places and outer space, rock out, and soar among the clouds with these other chapter book series from Little Bee Books!